WONDERS, INC.

by Crawford Kilian

illustrated by John Larrecq

PARNASSUS PRESS   BERKELEY, CALIFORNIA

for Alice

Early on a sunny summer morning, Christopher went walking down Main Street. "Everything looks just the same as yesterday, and the day before, and the day before that," he grumbled to himself.

There was Sam's Barber Shop. "I hate haircuts," Christopher growled.

There was Manny's Gas Station, with cars parked behind it. "I'd settle for a bike," said Chris.

There was Thompson's Dime Store. "Lamp shades and girls' stuff," snorted Christopher, although he was not above buying his kites there.

There was the Speedy-Shop Market. "Too many vegetables!"

And there was the Board of Education.

Chris could only shrug.

"What this town needs," he decided as he walked toward the meadows and the river, "is something new, something exciting."

He rounded a bend in the road and there, right in the middle
of the meadows, stood a factory. Thousands of rainbow-colored
windows gleamed in the sunlight, and ribbons of smoke streamed
from the chimneys. A spectacular sign above the factory read:
WONDERS, INC.

"Now, this," said Christopher, dazzled by the sight, "looks
more like it." He walked to the front gate, where a guard in a

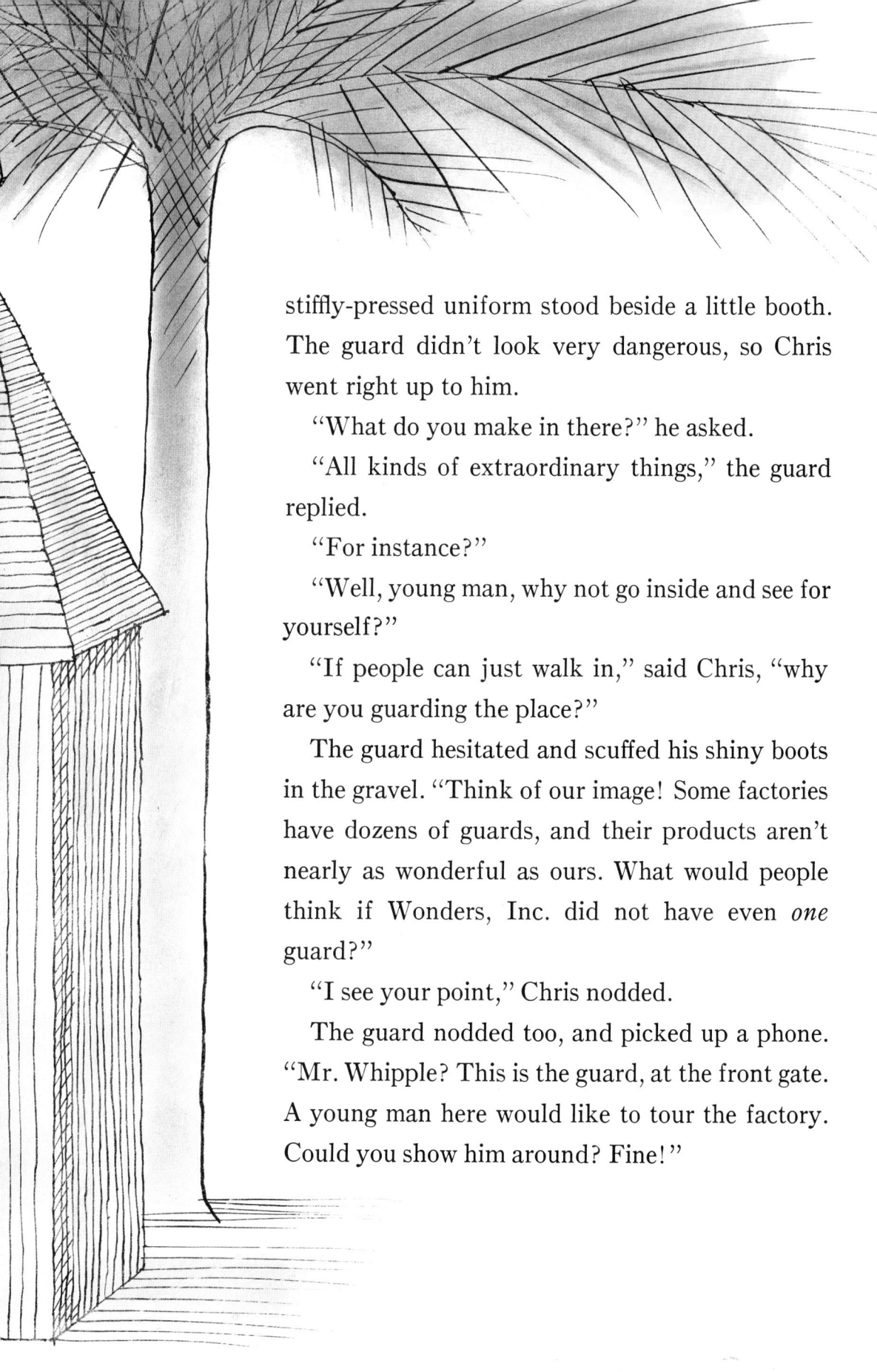

stiffly-pressed uniform stood beside a little booth. The guard didn't look very dangerous, so Chris went right up to him.

"What do you make in there?" he asked.

"All kinds of extraordinary things," the guard replied.

"For instance?"

"Well, young man, why not go inside and see for yourself?"

"If people can just walk in," said Chris, "why are you guarding the place?"

The guard hesitated and scuffed his shiny boots in the gravel. "Think of our image! Some factories have dozens of guards, and their products aren't nearly as wonderful as ours. What would people think if Wonders, Inc. did not have even *one* guard?"

"I see your point," Chris nodded.

The guard nodded too, and picked up a phone. "Mr. Whipple? This is the guard, at the front gate. A young man here would like to tour the factory. Could you show him around? Fine!"

A short, fat man came hurrying out of the factory. He skidded to a stop in front of Chris and held out his hand.

"Good morning, sir! I'm Mr. Whipple."

Chris shook his hand. "I'm Chris," he said.

"Very pleased to meet you, indeed. Well! You're our first visitor, and I hardly know where to begin."

"How about the line assembly?" the guard suggested.

"You mean the assembly line," Chris corrected him.

"No," beamed Mr. Whipple, "it's the line assembly, all right. Come along and I'll show you." He turned and trotted briskly toward the factory. The guard snapped to attention and saluted.

"Much obliged," said Chris, returning the salute. Then he hurried after Mr. Whipple, who was holding open a wide glass door.

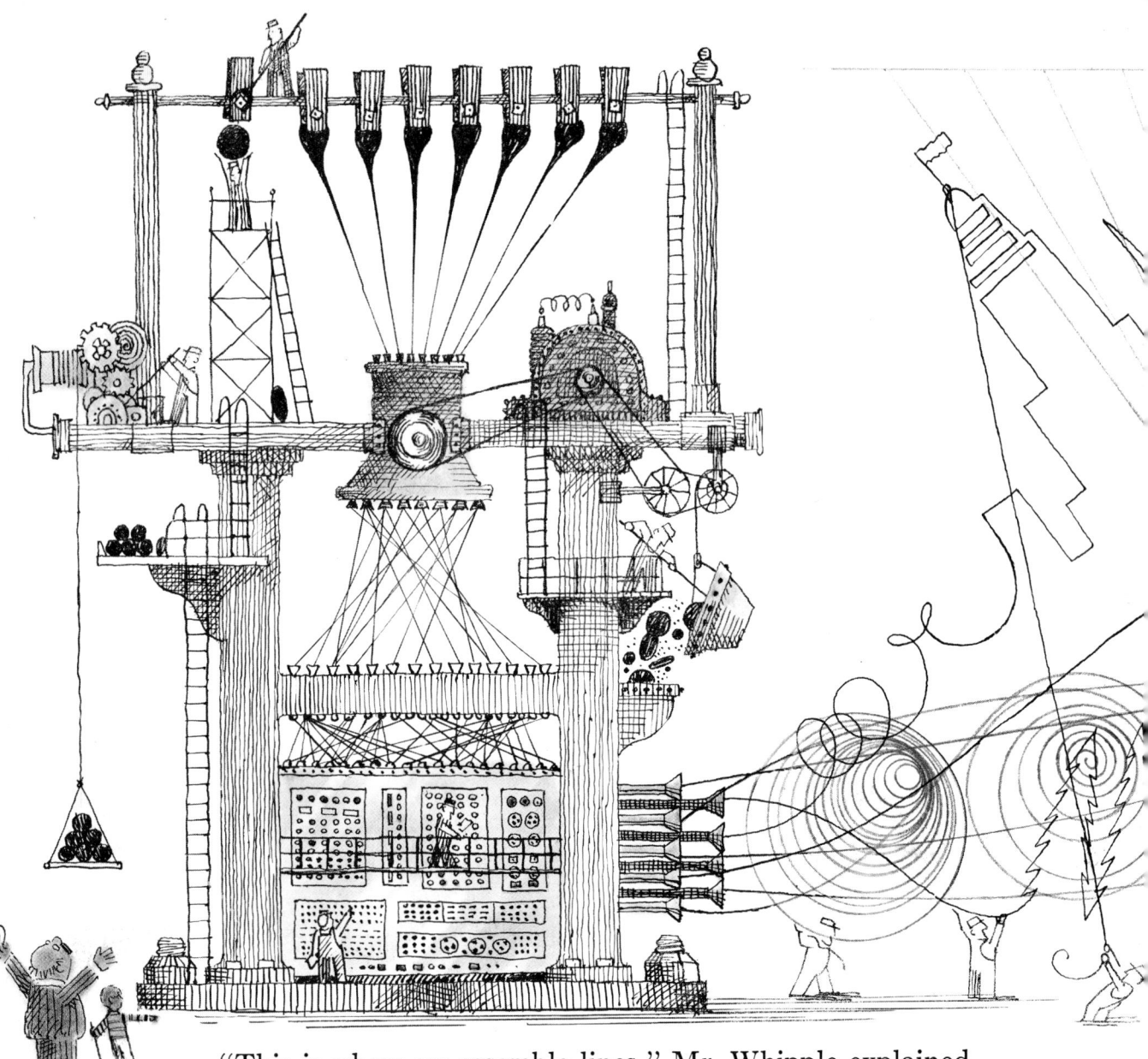

"This is where we assemble lines," Mr. Whipple explained, panting after his run. "We make the finest lines you can buy: skylines, hairlines, borderlines, sidelines, underlines, timber lines, and by-lines, to name just a few."

Chris's eyebrows went up. "How do you do it?"

"Simple," smiled Mr. Whipple. "We take a dot and stretch it. You can get four hundred feet of line from a single medium-sized

dot. Or, you can stretch it just a tiny bit and get a comma."

"What are those big vats for?"

"They are for boiling dots down to points. We produce compass points, points of order, jumping-off points, and counterpoints."

There was a loud *ping!* from one of the vats, and Mr. Whipple sighed. "That," he said, "was a point of no return."

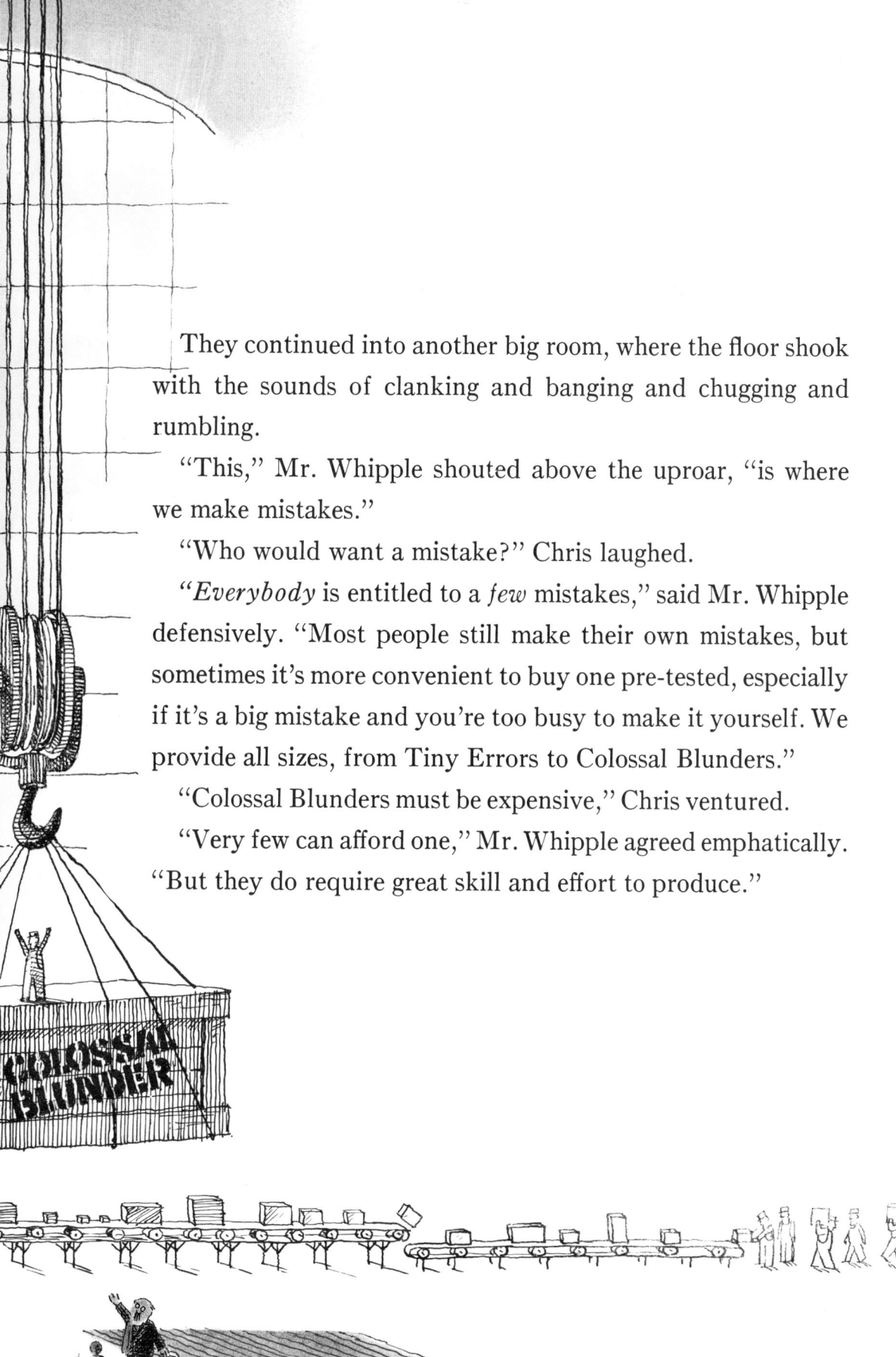

They continued into another big room, where the floor shook with the sounds of clanking and banging and chugging and rumbling.

"This," Mr. Whipple shouted above the uproar, "is where we make mistakes."

"Who would want a mistake?" Chris laughed.

"*Everybody* is entitled to a *few* mistakes," said Mr. Whipple defensively. "Most people still make their own mistakes, but sometimes it's more convenient to buy one pre-tested, especially if it's a big mistake and you're too busy to make it yourself. We provide all sizes, from Tiny Errors to Colossal Blunders."

"Colossal Blunders must be expensive," Chris ventured.

"Very few can afford one," Mr. Whipple agreed emphatically. "But they do require great skill and effort to produce."

Mr. Whipple quickly led the way into a long, low room where Chris heard a steady purr of clicking and ticking.

"Here we have the Clockworks, where we make time," said the plump little man. Chris looked at him suspiciously.

"Oh, I am serious, you know," exclaimed Mr. Whipple. "Time is one of our most popular products — nobody ever has enough of it."

"Well . . . maybe . . ." said Chris, still suspicious.

"Now, some people try to save time, some people can find time, and many people would like to borrow it. Even then, they waste most of it. We make all kinds of time!"

They walked among the machines, Mr. Whipple pointing

them out. "This one makes part-time; this one full-time; that one three-quarter time, time-and-a-half, and double-time. We also make Greenwich Mean Time, bedtime, pastime, nick-of-time, and a good variety of specialties."

"Specialties?" Chris repeated.

"Oh, yes. We turn out a fine brand of split seconds, not to mention fleeting moments and carefully-aged days. There's a great demand for the good old days, you know."

"Maybe among grownups," Chris added, "but I prefer nowadays."

"I thought you would. We make the best nowadays on the market."

The next room they entered
stretched as far as Chris could see.
"Here we are in the Space Mill. Time
needs space to flow through, as I'm
sure you've learned in school
along with the new math."
"Yes, we had that last year," Chris nodded,
trying to look in every direction at once.
"Well, our mill can produce any kind of space
you need. Outer space is quite popular today, but
our biggest seller is still closet space.
And we make a fine group of related products such as
elbow room, loopholes, and stop-gaps."

They walked toward one corner of the huge space room where the ceiling was almost lost in clouds of white balloons. "This is our flat space item — we sell most of these balloons to comic strip artists, who just write in the words."

"Why, they're as thin as paper," said Chris. He watched a man fill a balloon from a tank of helium and let it float up to the ceiling. "Mind if I fill one?" Chris asked.

"Not at all!" the man grinned. He handed Chris the hose from the tank and an empty balloon. Chris inflated the balloon with helium until it was more than twice his size and bobbed over his head. When he turned the balloon sideways, it almost disappeared.

"Be careful, now," warned Mr. Whipple. "They are very buoyant, so when you take it off the hose —"

But Chris had already released the balloon and immediately it began to float upward, with Chris holding on.

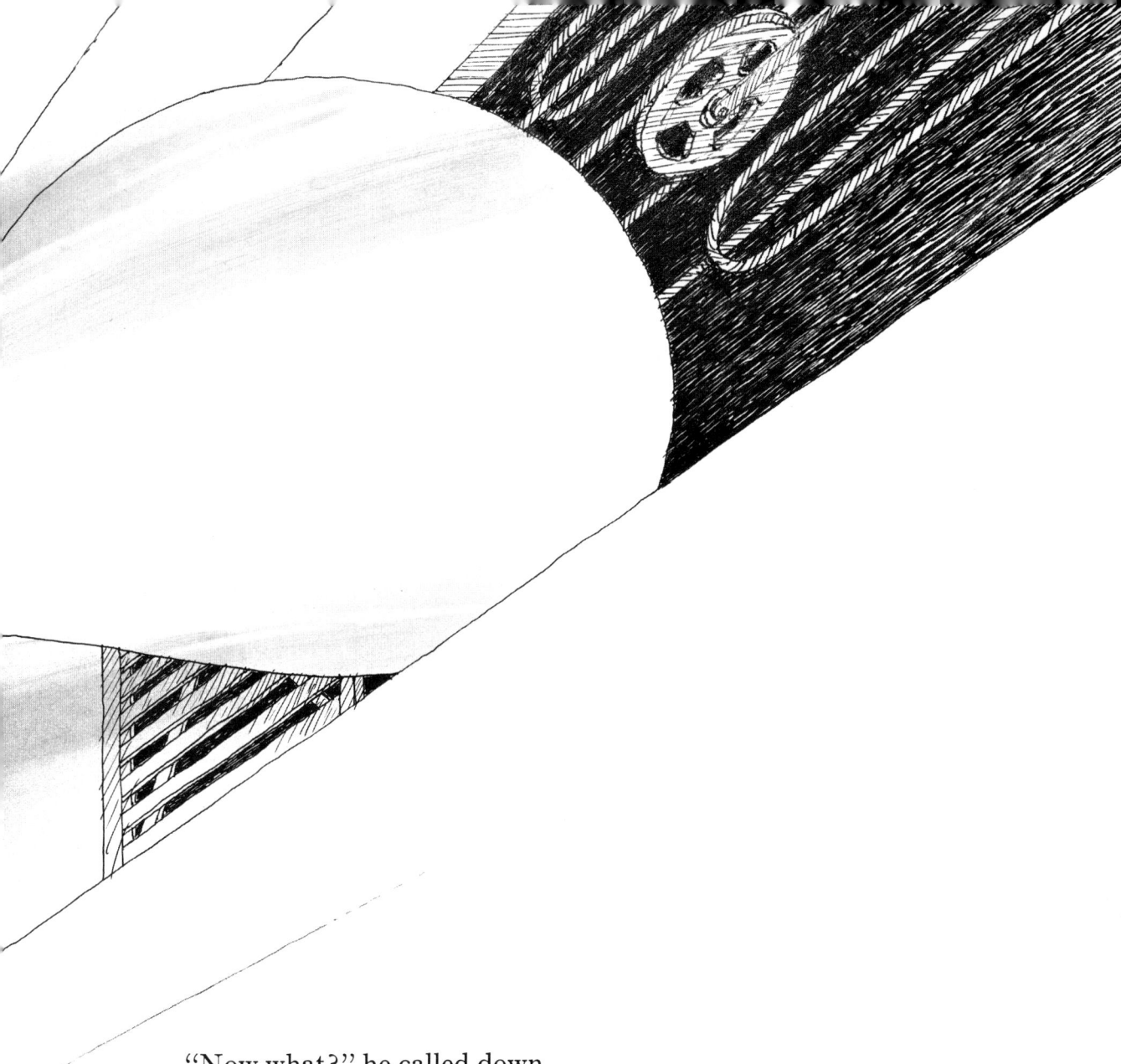

"Now what?" he called down.

"Hang on! Oh dear! Don't move, we'll bring a ladder!"

Chris's balloon, now caught in a draft, was soaring across the room. Mr. Whipple ran below with arms waving while Chris was carried up and away.

Suddenly it became darker, and the boy felt himself slowly rising up an elevator shaft. Before long he floated into a room where machines rang and sang and turned out delicate metal shapes. Workmen collected the metal shapes, dipped them in a pot of black paint, and hung them on long wires to dry.

"They look like musical notes," Chris said to himself, and when his foot caught on a wire the room was filled with music as the shapes clinked and tinkled. A man looked up in surprise and said: "Hey! No balloons allowed in here! This is the Music Hall!"

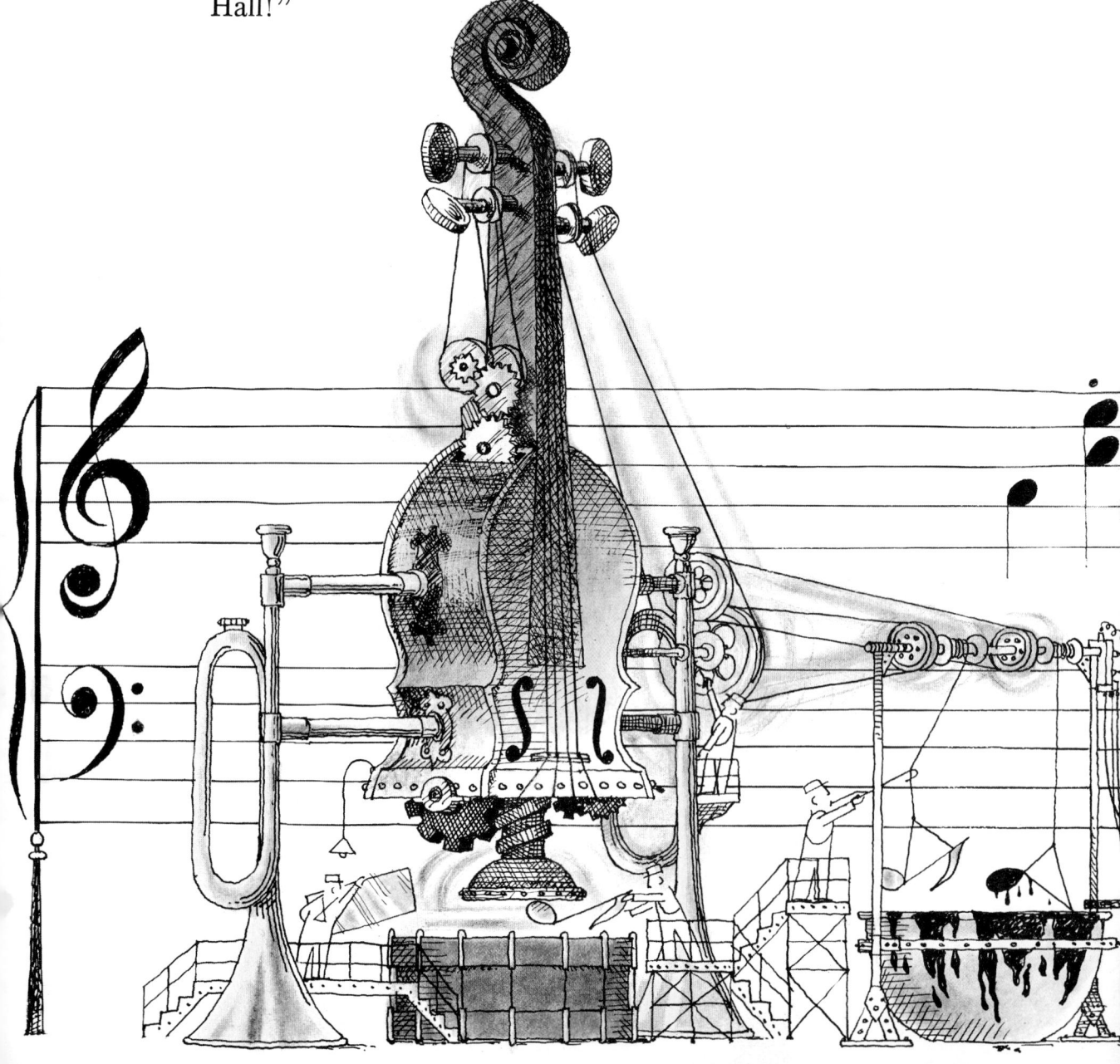

"Just what I thought," Chris called down, kicking his foot to free it from the wire. The notes all sang out again. "A very pretty tune," Chris added as he drifted on. "I think you've got a real hit."

"Thank you," the man beamed. "It's my latest composition. I'm the Senior Tunesmith. Now look out for the wood-winds ..."

It was too late. Chris felt a blast of melody and sawdust swirl

around him. He was pulled through a second elevator shaft and pushed out into a workshop of small cubicles where men were busy hammering and chiseling and carving.

"Hello down there!" Chris shouted. "Where am I?"

"This is the Word Department," answered a man wearing horn-rimmed glasses. "Are you in trouble?"

"No, but I would like to come down. Could you send for help?"

"No need to," laughed the man, picking up a dart-like object from his workbench. He aimed it carefully, then threw.

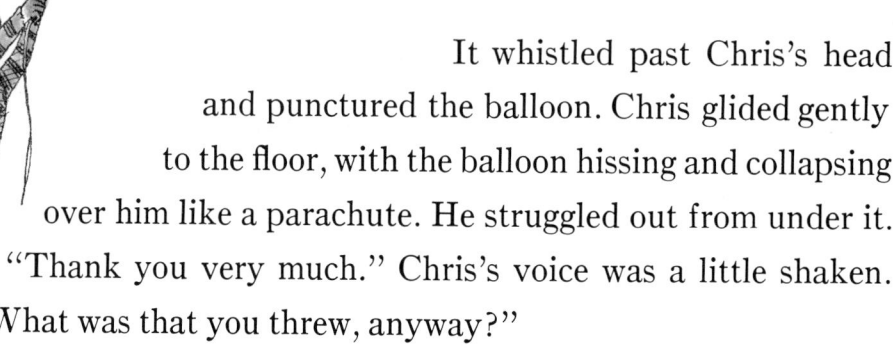

It whistled past Chris's head
and punctured the balloon. Chris glided gently
to the floor, with the balloon hissing and collapsing
over him like a parachute. He struggled out from under it.
"Thank you very much." Chris's voice was a little shaken.
"What was that you threw, anyway?"

The man pulled the object out of the balloon. "It's a Barbed
Wit," he said, holding it at arm's length. "A special craft of
mine. Horatio's my name, what's yours?"

"I'm Chris. I've been touring the factory, but I seem to have
lost my guide."

"Ah, yes. Mr. Whipple is looking for you over at the other
end of the shop. But let me show you
around while you're here."

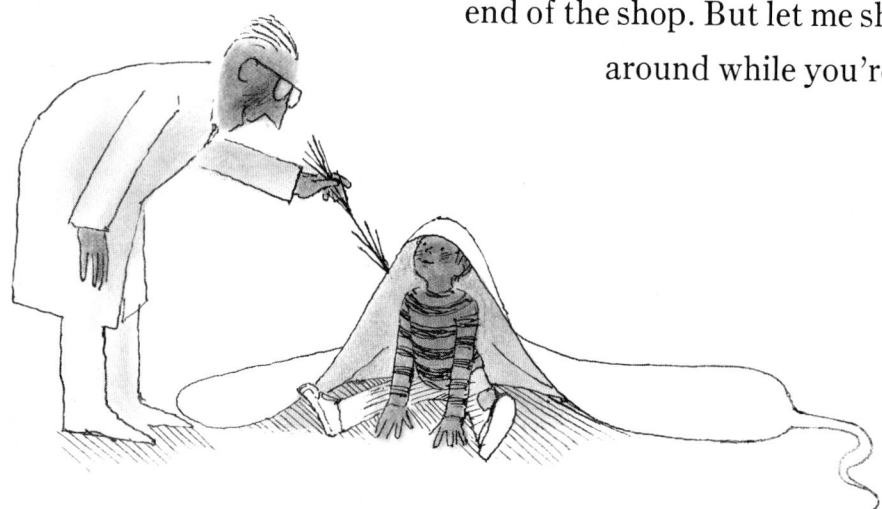

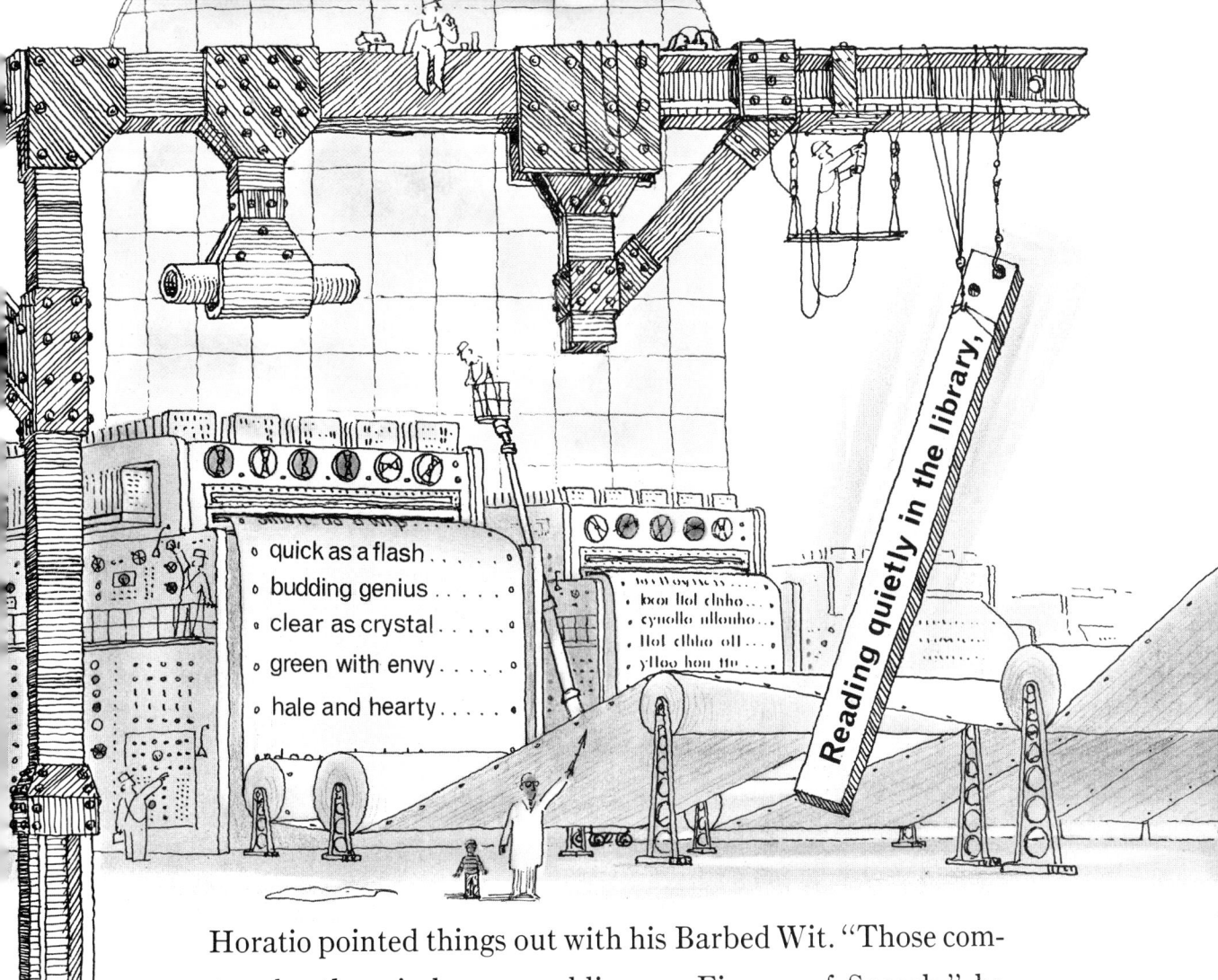

- quick as a flash . . . . .
- budding genius . . . . .
- clear as crystal . . . . .
- green with envy . . . . .
- hale and hearty . . . . .

Reading quietly in the library,

Horatio pointed things out with his Barbed Wit. "Those computers by the window are adding up Figures of Speech," he explained. "It used to take forever when we had clerks counting. Then we have the Proverbs Section; this machine can make anything from an ounce of prevention to a stitch in time. And that tank is used for mixing metaphors."

This gets better and better, Chris thought to himself. Then he asked, "What's that steel frame?"

"A sentence structure. It's not quite perfected; there is still a participle dangling from it."

"Tell me about the big apparatus over there," Chris pointed in another direction.

"With the lights and wires? Come and see it. This is our Verbotron! Biggest one in the country! Wonders, Inc. was first to split the infinitive, and the Verbotron did it."

Just then Mr. Whipple came puffing toward them, followed by a white-bearded old man wearing a well-tailored suit.

"Ah!" said Mr. Whipple. "Are you all right, Chris?"

"Yes, I'm fine Mr. Whipple. The balloon ride was fun."

"I'm so relieved! Words fail to express my relief . . ."

"I beg your pardon," Horatio interrupted rather stiffly, "but our words are guaranteed not to fail for five years or fifty thousand repetitions, whichever comes sooner."

"Of course, of course," Mr. Whipple murmured. "But, our very first visitor . . . I was at a loss . . ."

"We understand," said the bearded gentleman. "May I introduce myself, Chris? I'm the Chief Dreamwright."

"You write dreams?" asked Chris.

"The very best dreams," said Horatio loyally. "His daydreams get rave reviews, and his dreams of glory sometimes run for years." The old gentleman's face turned pink above his beard.

"I can't say I'm familiar with them," Chris said.

"Well, they are mostly for grownups," the Chief Dreamwright said, not at all offended. "Children prefer to make up their own dreams, and I admit they are much better at it than grownups."

His eyes twinkled and he looked at Chris thoughtfully. "I don't suppose you would care to accept a position as Junior Dreamwright, if we created a Children's Department, would you?"

"Umm . . . No, thanks," smiled Chris. "There just wouldn't be much of a demand, and anyway, I use all I can dream up.

But — I've been thinking . . . and of course I would have to clear it with Mother and Dad . . ."

"Yes?" said the Dreamwright, Mr. Whipple, and Horatio all together.

"I *would* consider a distributorship for the products of Wonders, Inc.," said Chris.

In no time the proposal was brought up before the Board of Directors and supported with great enthusiasm.

Christopher, with his parents' approval, was appointed distributor for Wonders, Inc. in his town, and his business is thriving.

He sells hairlines to Sam's Barber Shop;

a huge balloon advertises Manny's Gas Station.

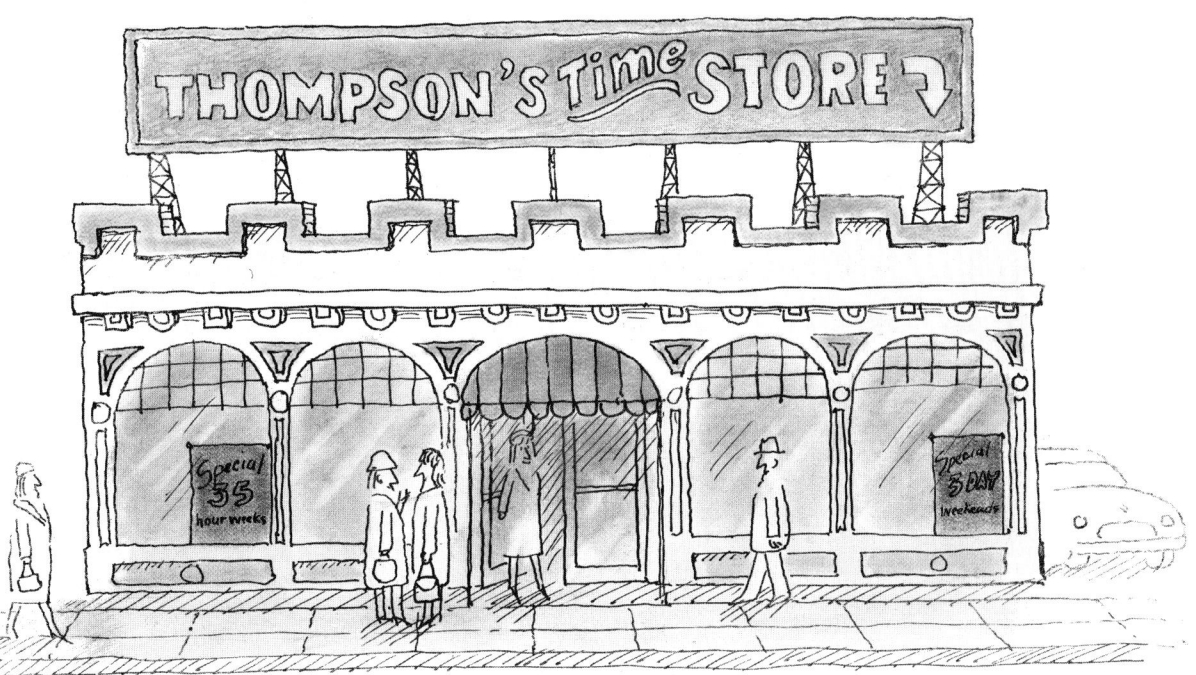

Thompson's Dime Store is now Thompson's Time Store, and
does a booming trade in thirty-five hour weeks and three-day
week-ends.

The Speedy-Shop Market still sells too many vegetables, but
the butcher has a word-mincer right next to his meat-grinder.

And every now and then, Chris sells a dream to the Board of Education.